Chesapeake Sleighride

Ram

Schooner

Illustrated by Joshua Tolford

Skipjack

Bugeye

CHESAPEAKE SLEIGHRIDE

Kenneth F. Brooks, Jr.

Chilton Book Company
Philadelphia   New York   London

Also by Kenneth F. Brooks, Jr.

RUN TO THE LEE

ISBN 0–8019–5549–1 Trade Edition
ISBN 0–8019–5550–5 Library Edition

Library of Congress Catalog Card Number 73–131237

This book is dedicated to my uncle, Thomas Aschom Gourley. It's nice to have uncles who know good stories.

Chesapeake Sleighride

Chapter One

"**Y**OU'RE NOT GOING to take that boy with you on a night like this, are you, John Talbott?"

Toby Wheeler watched closely as the man ignored the question until after he had finished drinking his coffee. He wiped his lips with his napkin, carefully folded it, rolled it, and slipped it into a silver napkin ring. Then he said, "I don't see why not. He's fourteen years old now. He's not a baby anymore. He aims to make his living as a sailor and going out on nights like this is part of being a sailor. *I'm* going and if I thought it was that all-fired dangerous I wouldn't go."

"I don't see why you're going either, for that matter. There's a blizzard out there and it's blowing a gale. It just doesn't make sense."

The man sighed. "I've just got to," he said. "I was born down there and you were too. You know how dependent those people are on the boats. And there hasn't been a boat go down the Bay in two weeks. Those people must be very short of coal, and the *Albatross* just happens to have a full load on board. I reckon I can get a pretty good price for it, and being the week before Christmas, God knows we can use the money. And I should be able to pick up a load of oysters down there and pick them up pretty cheap seein' as how nobody's been down there recently to buy any. And I oughta get a good price for them here in Baltimore when I get back, seein' as how nobody's come in with any oysters for two weeks and you know how people around here feel about oysters and Christmas. I'll bet there's not a fresh oyster in Baltimore."

"But we don't need the money, John. You know that."

"Didn't say we needed it, said we could use it, always can with three kids and this youngster to feed and clothe. And those people need coal. I just know they do. Tom Webster's got the *Hattie* loaded with

2

coal oil and he's going too. He doesn't think it's too dangerous."

The woman laughed. "That old fool," she said, but there was a gentle, loving tone in her voice. "He thinks he'll be lucky. Doesn't make any difference to him what the weather's doing as long as he feels lucky. One of these days his luck is going to catch up with him. You watch. One of these days."

"He's sixty-four and it hasn't caught up with him

yet. Besides, I don't believe in luck; you know that. I don't think luck's got anything to do with it. You plan well and things go well. There's no such thing as luck. My mother always told me that and by gosh, she was right."

The woman laughed again. "Next to me, she was the luckiest woman who ever lived. She had you for a son." She pushed her chair away from the table and got up. "Well, I know I can't stop you, and I wouldn't try if I could. But be careful, John. Christmas wouldn't be very much without you."

The man smiled. "I will be, Laura."

"And don't let Toby do anything dangerous."

"I won't," he said. He turned to the boy, whose eyes sparkled eagerly. "Come on, son, let's be on our way. Tide turns in about an hour and it'll take us that long to round up the rest of the crew and get under way."

They stepped out on the porch and waded through the snowdrifts until they reached the street. Toby looked back at the house, its windows warmly lighted, and thought it looked like a painting with the snow piled high on the evergreens and reflecting the light of the gas street lamp at the corner.

He fell into stride beside John Talbott and the two walked briskly toward the harbor where the tall schooners and rams and pungies and bugeyes were tied along the waterfront, snow drifting down quietly through their rigging. And just a few feet higher, out of the lee of the buildings, half a gale roared in out of the northeast. Nothing was moving on the Bay, and nothing, except for a small amount of inbound ocean commerce, had moved for two weeks as one blizzard after another hurled itself across the Eastern Shore and battered the crippled city.

The old-timers shook their heads and wondered. They had never seen such weather before, but the children played and frolicked, building snow forts and snowmen of remarkable endurance, while the ships stayed in port. The docks were filled with goods for shipment, and certain items were in very short supply.

As they walked through the snow toward the waterfront, Toby was excited and eager, but a little worried too. He was having a hard time making himself believe that this was really happening, that they were actually going to leave the harbor on such a night and go down the Bay. In the five years he had sailed on the *Albatross* they had never gone out in the face of such weather. Of course, most of his sailing had been done during the summer months

5

because of school, but even so, he couldn't remember any time the *Albatross* had set sail in weather such as this, and even if he had not gone himself he would have remembered. This was a night when most schooner captains would be found in their easy chairs before a roaring fire.

He knew there must be some very good reason for making the trip and he was curious to know what it was, but he was having a hard time finding the words to ask. He didn't want to sound as though he were questioning the skipper's judgment. He had never once felt any doubt about the wisdom and good judgment in anything John Talbott did, and he knew there was something more than money that was sending his skipper down the Bay that night.

For five years Toby had been a member of the Talbott family and he thought he knew the skipper pretty well. The *Albatross* was his real home, but in port—between trips and during the school term—he lived with the Talbotts, who had taken him off the streets when his mother died. Laura Talbott had been more of a mother to him than his own.

He had come aboard when nine as an unneeded cabin boy, although he had not known this at the time. But as he grew older he realized that the *Albatross* had never had a cabin boy before, and when he grew out of the job she was without one again.

The first day he was aboard, the skipper had pointed out the fact that he would not always be a cabin boy, and had fired his imagination by telling him that he might be a Bay captain someday. And he said something else that Toby had never forgotten: "Always remember this one thing when you get to be a captain. You are the captain because you can do any dirty, tough job on your boat better than any of the crew. And if you can, and they know you can, they will respect you and follow you anywhere, and you will never sail with an empty berth."

Toby had stood at the side of a master captain for five years and because he was a bright youngster, he had learned by watching, listening, and asking questions. He had learned to do every backbreaking task that came along and had learned to do them better than anyone else on the boat. He knew more at fourteen than most forecastle hands along the waterfront knew after more years at sea than they could count. And all the while he was absorbing more of the lifetime of lore and knowledge stored in the mind of John Talbott.

At eleven Toby began to do some of the work of a deckhand. He quickly learned to splice and crown a rope and to pull his own weight on a halyard. A short time later he was standing a regular trick at the wheel, and by the time he reached his fourteenth birthday in August just past he was making some of the landings in the quiet creeks where the *Albatross* called for cargo.

It was a hard life, for the sea is a tough mistress, and a ninety-foot schooner is demanding—and unforgiving of even the slightest inattention—but as he looked back on that life he knew it had been wonderful and exciting too. There had been times when his labors had left him exhausted, but there had never been a time when they had soured him.

At fourteen he was a big boy and growing steadily. John Talbott had expressed the opinion that he would reach six feet three before he stopped growing. He was already close to five eleven and had shoulders like a stevedore's and muscles in his arms and legs like Manila hawsers.

He had grown wise and strong in the ways of the Bay. He knew the pitfalls and the havens, the currents and the caprices of the weather. In spite of his age he was a seasoned, valuable young man who knew the day would come when he could rely on himself to exercise command.

And he suddenly realized that he had learned a great deal of what he knew by asking questions.

John Talbott had never resented nor grown impatient with any of his questions. It was obvious to Toby he was being trained for future command. *There must be something I don't understand about this,* he thought. *And I reckon it's something I ought to know.*

He glanced at the skipper and cleared his throat. "Skipper, are we really going down the Bay tonight?"

"Why not?" The answer was not a curt cutoff but an obvious invitation for him to expound his views.

"Well, Skipper, I don't know, but it seems to me like a hell of a night and I don't see a lot of other boats leaving the harbor."

"Tom Webster's taking the *Hattie* out tonight. He's going with us."

"He's really going then?"

"That's right. We're going together."

"How far are we going, Skipper?"

"Solomons, if we can get in there. If we can't we'll go to the mouth of the Potomac. Maybe to the Rappahannock. I don't know. All depends on how it goes."

"Skipper, would I be out of line if I asked why? Why tonight?"

"No. I want you to ask about anything you don't

understand and you couldn't understand about this because I haven't told you. I've been looking at the barometer readings and back over the log, studying the weather we've been having, and I think we're due for a big break. I think it's going to break later on tonight or early tomorrow. Top's going to blow off and we'll have a brisk, fine northwester. That's what I think.

"Now, if we wait until tomorrow to see if I'm right, every boat in this harbor will be out of here and a cargo of coal won't bring what it'll bring if we're the first boat to get there. And a cargo of oysters won't bring as much, either, if everybody's coming up the Bay with a load of them. It's a chance to pick up a good profit at both ends.

"But, Toby, I was born and raised down there and I know a lot of those people. And I figure a lot of them are getting short of coal and some of them are cold. They're counting on somebody to get through to them soon or they'll be in real trouble. Maybe some of them already are. I think we should try, and I think this is the time to try."

They had reached the intersection of Light and Pratt streets and stopped in the middle to turn and face into the teeth of the gale. As John Talbott turned his head from side to side, feeling the wind on his sensitive earlobes, he thought he detected a slight shift. "North-northeast," he muttered. "But still blowing half a gale."

Standing there on the snow-covered street, John Talbott would have presented somewhat of a problem to the inland city dweller seeking to describe him, but looking at him, Toby Wheeler would have had no trouble at all. He would have simply described him as a waterman and felt that this was adequate. He had the face of a man somewhat older than his forty-two years. It had a leathery, deeply lined look about it, but it was a face that smiled easily, and his eyes were the clearest blue imaginable. All in all, however, smile or no, it was a face that could best be described as determined, and even the casual observer would have known that this was the face of a man secure in the knowledge that he was competent to stand up against anything that might be thrown at him.

The rest of his body, however, was not at all like that of an older man or even that of the usual man his age. Beneath the warm clothing he was wearing was the body of a young athlete in top physical condition. He was six feet tall, powerfully built, with heavily muscled arms and legs that had been developed by years aloft in the rigging and straining at

11

the end of a hawser or halyard. And he carried himself with an air of dignity and determination that radiated to all those around him and made men willing to follow him anywhere.

After studying the wind for several minutes, he turned and walked with the boy down the street toward the dock where the *Albatross* was moored.

Almost the moment they stepped on the deck the forecastle hatch opened and Harry Bailey stuck his head out and looked aft across the deck. He had felt the first footfall on the gangplank even though it was cushioned with snow. Harry was one of the two forecastle hands on the *Albatross,* a twenty-one-year-old whose father had tried to force him to be a banker in Indianapolis. He had run away from his father's bank for a more adventuresome life. Unlike the rest of the crew, he lived full time aboard the *Albatross,* making his home in the small, pie-shaped cabin wedged into the bow, two thirds belowdecks, covered by a low deckhouse.

Harry hadn't really believed all the earlier talk about going down the Bay. He was certain it was some kind of fancy joke someone was playing on someone else, although he wasn't quite sure what parties were actually involved. He hadn't gone quite so far as to pull off his outer clothing and climb into his bunk, but he was about to when he became aware of someone's coming aboard.

He tossed aside the reef point he was backsplicing and climbed the ladder out of the forecastle, shoved back the hatch, and came up on deck. He walked aft, peering through the snow, and made out the shape of John Talbott. Toby Wheeler was with him.

"Bull come aboard yet, Harry?" Captain Talbott asked.

"No, sir, not yet. I went up to his house like you said, and told him we'd be sailing tonight. Told him what time the tide was going to turn and told him you wanted to sail then. He said he'd be here. Looked like he was lookin' forward to it."

"Well, he should be along shortly."

Harry noted the expectancy in the skipper's voice. *Maybe he really meant it,* he thought. "Are we sailing, Skipper?" he asked.

"That's right. Now let's look alive and start getting ready to cast off. Who's that coming through the snow?"

"Looks like Captain Webster," Toby said. The boy was right and soon Captain Webster was climbing the gangplank. He was a short, heavyset man with big shoulders and a bushy white beard. He

13

spoke with a soft voice that sounded on the verge of laughter most of the time. He stepped down on the deck and approached John Talbott. "You about ready to go?"

"We'll be ready shortly. Anybody else showing any signs of moving?"

Captain Webster shook his head. "I walked up and down the docks and everything is quiet. I don't think we're going to have any company, but I do think it would be a good idea if we hung together out there tonight instead of trying to make a race out of it. If you agree, and want to do likewise, I'll hang a lantern in my yawl davits so we can keep each other in sight. If we do that there won't be much chance of us running together. But I'll tell you this: you'll have to find your own way back because I'm not going to sit around down there waiting for you." He turned and started down the gangplank. Halfway down he stopped and turned around. "Send Toby down to let me know when you're ready to go." He paused, standing there in the driving snow. "And, John, I've got a ten-dollar gold piece that says I get back first."

"That's a bet," John Talbott said happily. He turned and looked up the street. "Here comes Bull now. The tide turns at 10:42. We've got fifteen minutes. Let's get moving."

14

"Yes, sir," Harry Bailey said as he watched Ed Shorter come up the gangplank. "Hear that, Bull?" Harry said. "We're getting ready to sail. We'll find out what kind of a sailor you are tonight. I'll bet when you were rounding the Horn you never saw anything like we're going to see tonight." He said it loudly enough for John Talbott to hear it, and there was a slight note of reproach in his voice, but the skipper had struck a match and was studying the thermometer on the binnacle; if he heard it he gave no sign.

Ed Shorter stepped down onto the deck and slapped Toby on the shoulder. "Well, young fellow, you'll really get a chance to see what it's like tonight."

Toby caught a glimpse of his face in the light from the gas street lamp at the end of the dock. Bull was smiling. It was a very gentle smile for such a hard-looking man. He had a leathery face, deeply tanned in spite of the month of the year, friendly eyes, and that easy grace of a big man who knows he has nothing to fear or prove. He had spent thirty years in full-rigged ships out of Hamburg, Germany, making the trip around the Horn and up to the nitrate ports of Peru three times a year. Baltimore-born, he had come in on a ship two years back and decided to stay awhile. Once aboard the *Al-*

batross he decided Bay sailing was more in keeping with his forty-eight years than the howling blasts and high seas of the South Atlantic.

Toby went to work knocking the snow off the sails, freeing the stops, and lighting the running lights, all the time watching for the moment when the boats at anchor would swing around into the ebb tide. He went below for a few moments and came up with a freshly filled, clear white lantern, which he lighted. He climbed over the stern railing and out onto one of the davits that lifted the yawl boat out of the water. Resting one knee on the bow of the small boat hanging there, he used a short piece of stop cord to secure the lantern.

He worked his way back down the davit and climbed back over the rail. He dropped to the deck and again looked out over the harbor. Just as he did he saw one of the boats anchored a short distance away swing around into the ebb tide. He heard the skipper's voice: "Toby, go tell Cap'n Tom we're ready to sail."

Chapter Two

At 10:42 THE TWO schooners cast off and eased down the channel toward Seven Foot Knoll. The ebb tide had started to run just as they drifted away from the sheltered wharf, and as Toby pushed against the corner pile in an effort to swing the *Albatross* clear he had the strangest feeling that he'd like to wrap his arms around that pile and hold onto it all night long. As he took his hand away he felt as though he had said good-bye to the world for a while. He had never felt that way before.

As he trimmed the mainsail he looked out over

the stern and watched the riding light of a big freighter anchored in the channel fade away into the gloom astern, then turned to peer ahead through the snow, his eyes fixed on the lantern ahead. The *Hattie* had been moored a hundred feet downstream and was leading the way.

Before the *Albatross* was fifteen minutes out a thin crust of snow had matted on the front of Toby's heavy winter coat. He beat at it with his hands but accomplished little. He noticed that the front of the skipper's coat also was matted with snow and, as if acting on his suggestion, John Talbott began to beat at the ice crust to knock it away. His efforts were no more effective than Toby's.

Off the port bow a light flashed—hardly more than a glow through the driving snow. "That'll be Lazarette," Talbott said. "Take a good look at it, boys, because it's probably the last light you'll see for a while except for that lantern of Tom Webster's." Toby watched the flashing light as it dropped astern.

"We'll change the helm every hour, Toby," the skipper said. "Every hour on the hour." He turned to Harry Bailey, who had the wheel. "So you get a short trick to start. I'll take the wheel for a minute while you go get Bull to relieve you." He turned back to Toby. "You think you can take a regular trick on this trip? It's a rough night, son."

There was no question in Toby's mind as he answered eagerly, "Yes, sir!"

"All right, your trick will start at midnight. One hour on and two hours off—Harry, Bull, and you. If it gets too tough I'll spell you."

The skipper took the wheel, wrapping his big fingers around the spokes, feeling the rudder kick against his hands. He looked aloft into the high rigging, wondering about the upper blocks and the jaws of the main gaff, but he was unable to make out anything because of the darkness and the snow. He was very much worried about something freezing up there.

The clear white lantern hanging in the yawl davits gave him some light on the mainsail and he studied the set of the sail intently, paying particular attention to the luff, the side running up the mast, searching for any flutter that might indicate he was sailing too close to the wind. It was a tight beat out of the channel, which ran generally southeast, with the wind from the northeast, but the *Albatross* was at her best sailing close to the wind. Most boats, sailing close-hauled, with the sails trimmed flat, could sail about forty-five degrees off the wind, but the *Albatross* would sail a few degrees closer to the wind, meaning that she would make a little more distance to windward on every tack than the average schooner.

The skipper nodded to Ed Shorter as he stepped to the wheel. "We have us a bird dog tonight, Bull." He pointed off to the lantern. "Stay with him. Follow that light."

An hour later, at exactly midnight, as though it had been geared in with the ship's clock striking eight bells, the wind suddenly freshened, the boat heeled sharply to starboard, and the spray smashed back across the deck. John Talbott turned and looked at Ed Shorter. The big man was smiling. It was a wide smile of pleasure. They had passed out from under the lee of North Point. They were now in the Chesapeake Bay and the welcome was not friendly.

At this precise moment, some fifty miles to the south, Seaman John Davis of the United States Coast Guard was climbing the spiral stairway to the top of Cove Point Lighthouse. He was making a regularly scheduled check of the lens and its operating mechanism. When he reached the top of the stairs he stood for a moment gazing out at the fingers of light that swept majestically around the lighthouse, each one sharply defined by the falling snow.

The lighthouse—a tall, circular, tapering white tower—had stood since 1828 on the western shore of the Chesapeake, at the mouth of the Patuxent River, on a point which, if one approaches it from the north, makes well out into the Bay. To the south the land falls away more gradually in a series of bluffs known as the Cliffs of Calvert, so named from the county in which they are located. The station was manned by the Coast Guard and was a reporting station for ocean commerce inbound for Baltimore.

Seaman Davis completed his check and went below to take over the midwatch. As he trudged through the snow from the tower to the radio shack, he was looking forward to a quiet night. So far as he knew, nothing was moving on the Bay. He relieved the watch, poured himself a cup of coffee, and sat down to wait until 8:00 A.M.

Toby came on deck only a moment after the ship's clock finished striking midnight. He looked around and then stepped over to take the wheel. He looked at Ed Shorter, whose coat and hat were covered with snow. "Rough night, isn't it?" he said.

"Aye," Ed replied. "But you can really drive her with this kind of steady wind blowing and that load

22

of coal we've got down there. With all the weight we're carrying belowdecks she'll smash her way right through almost anything."

Toby took the wheel and the older man stepped away. "Where's the skipper?"

"He's forward. Worried about everything icing up. Reminds me of the good old days, wind blowing a gale and water coming over the decks. Lad," he said, "when I was on the Potosí with Hilgendorf he used to load her down to the gunwales, almost no freeboard showing at all, and we'd smash our way through the seas down there around Cape Horn and she'd hardly raise her bow. She'd just smash right through. What a grand man he was! He was tough, but he was fair and he knew what he was doing and he wasn't scared of the weather or anything else. He was a driver. That's what I like about sailing with the skipper. He's a lot like that old man. We wouldn't be out here tonight if he wasn't. You can learn a lot from him, Toby, and when your time comes you'll be ready."

The skipper came aft. He and Ed Shorter went below: John Talbott to his cabin to quickly plot his position on the chart and return on deck; Bull to the galley for some hot coffee to warm his insides.

At twelve-twenty, following the light on Tom

23

Webster's stern, the *Albatross* swung slightly to the south and wallowed in the heavy seaway. Ed Shorter and Harry Bailey came on deck quickly to retrim the sails. The wind was now directly abeam and instead of smashing through the waves the boat was sailing in the troughs, rolling heavily as the waves passed under her. Spray still broke over the deck and at times the long bowsprit plunged into the sea, but the change in course gave the impression that the wind had eased. The men relaxed ever so slightly. "We've passed Seven Foot Knoll," the skipper said. "I didn't see the light and I doubt if Tom Webster saw it either, but I figure he turned just right."

Toby stood on the windward side of the wheel, his body leaning into the roll of the boat, his hands on the spokes, his head thrust forward as he studied the movements of the men on deck, at the same time watching the set of the mainsail and the light on the *Hattie.* He felt a thrill go through him as the *Albatross* battled the storm. The night was cold and raw and it was downright uncomfortable to be out in weather like this. If he had been ashore he would have thought twice about even stepping outdoors except to go sledding, but the liveness of this experience, the sounds and smells and movements, were so exciting that the discomfort was unimportant. He thought about his classmates back in the warmth of their homes, probably long in bed by now. He didn't envy them at all. Wouldn't he have something to talk about when school reopened after the holidays!

The bow of the *Albatross* was pointed almost straight down the Bay. The wind was far around on the port quarter, although not coming directly over the stern. The boat was yawing and pitching, her tall masts scribing great circles in the ceiling of snow. It was snowing much harder, the wind screamed through the frozen rigging, and the sickening lurch that came with each overtaking wave left little doubt that the storm was mounting in fury. The wind was almost straight out of the north and very close to a whole gale. Toby was glad they had come out with a double reef in the mainsail, no foresail, and a big reef in the jib.

The bow of the *Albatross* was now plunging into every wave, and at times it seemed to Toby that she might be driven under. Rivers of water poured astern each time her bow came up. Some of it ran down the deck and poured out the scuppers and back into the Bay. Some of it froze to the lower rigging. And some of it formed a thin sheet of ice on the deck. Moving around became very hazardous and Toby wondered how he could have thought, less than a half hour ago, that the wind was easing. He wondered how the crew on the *Hattie* were standing up to the tortures of the night.

When the two boats had changed course near Seven Foot Knoll, the *Albatross* had been riding about thirty yards aft of the *Hattie* on her port quarter, but on the reach that followed, with her centerboard raised slightly, she had drawn up inch by inch until she was now directly abeam, with a scant twenty yards separating the two schooners. Toby could see the *Hattie*'s port running light, a diffuse red glow, rising and falling through the snow. He could hear the crashing rush of water between the two boats.

John Talbott was also aware of the fact that he was gradually gaining on the other and was pleased with the knowledge that the *Albatross*'s speed would stand him in good stead on the way home. He hoped the *Hattie* was also sailing with her board partially raised, since this was the only fair way to compare the two boats, and he was sure she was. He couldn't imagine Tom Webster's not taking advantage of the following wind in this manner. He took the wheel and told Toby to go below and lower the board slightly. He had no desire to pass Captain Webster and the *Hattie* and lose them in the night.

He knew clearly in his mind what his action would be upon reaching the mouth of the Patuxent. He would be almost up under the stern of the *Hattie* at that time, maybe a little to port, with his crew ready. He would figure it as closely as he could, attempting to get the jump on the *Hattie*'s crew. He would jibe under her stern, blanket her wind as he passed, his sail blocking the wind and causing her to lose headway, then slip around Drum Point and run for Cook's Wharf, taking the inside channel. If he could beat the *Hattie* to the dock, he would unload immediately. It would have to be a fast operation, and he hoped he could get a wharf crew working with him before Tom Webster came in. Loose coal always made slower unloading than barrels of coal oil.

He knew that even if the boats started back at the same time he had the faster boat. He knew from past experience that she would sail closer to the wind. He only hoped he had the skill to overcome Tom Webster's experience and cunning. He knew it would be a boat race all the way up the Bay.

While John Talbott was planning his strategy,

Toby Wheeler was attending to the centerboard. This big board was actually a part of the *Albatross*'s keel and kept her from being blown sideways by anything other than a following wind. It was raised and lowered, depending on how much of it was needed, and was a necessity because Bay schooners went into many small creeks and harbors where the water was too shallow for a keel boat.

Toby welcomed the respite below, where it was warmer than out on the exposed deck. He was surprised at how tired he had become after a little less than an hour at the wheel. He found that handling the big schooner in the heavy weather called for sharpness and skill, and the weather wore hard on the man at the wheel, slowing his reflexes and sapping the strength needed to hold the boat on her course. The other men on deck could move around, flap their arms, and stomp their feet, but he had been a fixed target for the snow and icy spray as he stood poised and tense, rigidly holding the spokes of the wheel, his eyes fixed on that white lantern ahead.

When he finished lowering the board slightly he shut the small doorway in the front bulkhead of the aft cabin. He turned and looked at Harry Bailey, who was just pouring himself a cup of steaming coffee. "Just trying to get good and warm before I take the wheel," Harry said with a smile. "It sure is cold up there."

Toby nodded and watched as Harry took a sip of his coffee and made a face at it. He put the cup down slowly on the counter and held it there to keep it from sliding.

"Too hot?" Toby asked.

Harry shook his head. "No. I don't know what's wrong with it. I know it's good coffee, but it sure doesn't taste good to me."

Harry had been in the cabin for about twenty minutes making that pot of coffee, and the longer he stayed the more conscious he was of the heat and the stuffiness. As he set the cup down he was aware that nothing would taste very good to him at this particular moment. Sweat was breaking out on his forehead, his face felt flushed, and his stomach was very unsettled. He took another sip of the coffee, quickly spit it into the sink, emptied his cup after it, and hung the cup on a hook overhead. He rubbed his hand across his forehead. "I don't know what's wrong with me, Toby. I've never been seasick in the year I've been aboard, but I feel like I'm gonna be now. It sure feels hot in here, doesn't it?"

"Maybe you ought to get back on deck," Toby said. "Nothing better for that kind of feeling than fresh air and there's lots of it up there."

Harry needed no further urging. He headed for the deck. He had an overwhelming urge to get some fresh air.

Toby came up just behind him, prepared to take the wheel again, but the skipper had given it to Harry. "Your time was up anyway, so let's go below for a few minutes. I've got to check our position and you should get something warm in your stomach and rest awhile." He turned to Harry. "Follow that light, son. Stay right with him. I'll be back in a few minutes."

Toby followed the skipper down into the aft cabin and pulled the hatch shut after him. He trailed the skipper into his cabin and stood beside him at the long table where the chart was laid out. He always loved to watch John Talbott work out his position. "Why do you need to do that?" Toby asked. "As long as we're following Tom Webster, why do we need to figure out our position?"

"Let me tell you something, son," the skipper said. "When you're following somebody else it's always a good idea to know where you're going. Because if you lose him, or if he begins to go astray, at least you know where you are. In a lot of cases even if you don't know where you are, if you know how you got there you have a chance of finding your way back. Although I can't say I'd like to chance going back into Baltimore harbor tonight."

Toby watched the skipper as he consulted with his clock, chart, and parallel rule, arriving at a position based on dead reckoning, plus a certain amount of God and guess—tide about so much, give or take a little because the wind was pushing on the waves; course about so much, since it was impossible to steer a precise course in such heavy weather; and time, exactly for a change, so much. With these estimates he drew his course line on the chart and, using his dividers, ticked off the miles, hoping for compensating errors that would somehow balance out instead of errors that would compound the slightest miscalculation into one huge catastrophe that would cast him ashore.

He placed a mark on the chart, wrote "1 A.M." alongside it, and put his dividers and rule back in the drawer. He patted Toby on the shoulder, said, "Get some rest," and returned to the deck.

As he stepped back on deck at 1:10 he looked off to port into the snow as if he expected by some miracle to see the light at Love Point, which they were passing at this moment, according to his calculations. Even though he could not see it, he knew exactly what it looked like, just as he knew what the shores of Gibson Island looked like on the starboard side. He had seen all of this so many times in his life. He turned forward and took a turn around the deck to check the running tackle. A thin coat of ice was forming on everything and he knew he'd have to do something about that.

Seaman John Davis looked up at the clock. The time was dragging. He had had the watch for only one hour and ten minutes, but it seemed like all night. He was deep in the study of *The Elements of Navigation*, by W. J. Henderson. Davis was an ambitious young man who hoped to make a career out of the Coast Guard service, and he studied constantly to improve his knowledge. He reread the paragraph in front of him: "Remember that you can never be too sure of your position. Eternal vigilance is the price of safety at sea, and dangers increase with the approach to land."

His roommate, until recently stationed at Cape Hatteras, was full of stories that bore testimony to the accuracy of this statement. Also he remembered reading of a Spanish steamer, *Príncipe de Asturias,* that had struck a rock off Sebastien Point in the spring with the loss of 500 lives.

Chapter Three

Toby Wheeler steadied himself against the roll of
the boat and carefully poured himself a cup of
coffee. This was one of the things he liked about
sailing on the *Albatross.* He could drink coffee as
the men did. He never got any coffee ashore. Laura
Talbott thought he was far too young to be drinking
coffee. It would damage his nerves and stunt his
growth.

He was standing in the galley, such as it was, on
the starboard side of the aft cabin, just forward of
the captain's quarters. It was a very small room,

large enough for a coal stove on gimbals that kept the stove level no matter what the boat did. It was not a large stove but was ample for the meals cooked on board during trips. There were also an icebox—holding 200 pounds of ice—storage space for staples, and a sink. The sink had a pump that drew in seawater which was used for washing dishes, and when the stopper was pulled the water ran down a pipe and out an opening in the hull. The galley was the province of Harry Bailey, who did all the cooking for the crew.

The galley was separated by a counter from the area where the crew ate. The eating area, which had no formal name, was never called anything in particular by the crew. It was certainly not called the dining saloon or the wardroom or anything else that might serve as a title on a larger ship. This area and the galley formed the forward half of the aft cabin.

To enter it, a man came down the aft companionway, walked along the passageway between the captain's cabin and that occupied by Toby Wheeler when he was aboard, and on into the dining room. It had one window in the forward part of the cabin trunk—that part above the level of the deck—and two on the port side. There was also a pair of windows in the galley, which occupied the starboard side of the area. All these windows were tightly sealed and caulked to keep out the spray and were never opened.

Most of the ventilation came from two scoop-shaped funnels that went up through the ceiling and were turned one way or the other, depending on the weather and on the necessity to keep out the spray or rain or snow, in which case their faces were turned away from the wind. They could be turned to face into the wind if it was cool and dry. There was also a skylight directly over the middle of the cabin, and this was opened in good weather.

Toby leaned against the counter, his knees flexed, steadying himself against the wild rolling motion of the *Albatross,* and tried to drink his coffee without spilling it. *Harry sure did look funny,* he thought. His face had been as red as a beet. Funny, it didn't seem hot to Toby down there—just nice and warm. He wished he could stay there all night. A little fresh air ought to do the trick though. He certainly hoped it would because Harry was up there on deck right now holding the wheel.

The relative quiet of the cabin was broken by the sounds of outside noises and he knew someone had opened the hatch to come below. He leaned across the counter and looked down the passageway. It was the skipper and he was motioning to Toby. "Can you come on deck, son? I need you."

Toby gulped the rest of his coffee, tossed the cup into the sink, and hurried on deck. He looked around in amazement, dismayed by the change that had taken place in the twenty-five minutes he had been below. The *Albatross* was a floating drift of snow, or so it seemed. She had the shape of a boat, but none of the details of her rigging, running tackle, or deck gear showed as such. All of it took on a fuzzy shape, and the windlasses, cleats, and chocks were only mounds of snow. He saw the skipper standing near the wheel. The two looked at each other for several seconds. "Snowing, ain't it, skipper?"

"It sure is, Toby. Harder than it was when we left the slip. A lot harder, I'd say, but maybe it's just that the wind is driving it so hard."

"It wasn't sticking to her like it is now," the boy said. "Not even half an hour ago it wasn't."

"I know. I wonder when it's going to stop!"

"I wonder *if* it's going to stop."

"I know."

"Glad the *Hattie*'s still in sight," Toby said as he looked at the light, more of a glow than a light, in the snow just forward off the starboard bow.

"Yep, and I hope to God she stays in sight. It's a comfort to know she's there. Reminds me there's someone else who's as big a fool as I am."

The boy laughed. "Also someone who thinks we're on course. Don't forget that, Skipper. Where are we?"

"Well, I figure we passed Love Point about——" he leaned around and looked at the clock on the binnacle housing just below the compass "——thirty-five minutes ago. Ought to be about off the mouth of the Severn by now."

"Making good time, aren't we?"

"We oughta be, son. We've got everything in our favor. Wind fair and blowing a gale and the tide still ebb. We oughta be makin' time. I only hope we can stop when the time comes."

They both laughed. There was an easy give-and-take between them despite the difference in their ages. "Reason I called you up here, son, was because of all this stuff sticking to the running gear. See if you can clear some of it away, will you?"

"Yes, sir," Toby said. "There's fresh-made coffee below, Skipper. Why don't you go down and have yourself a cup and warm up for a couple minutes? I'll keep an eye on things up here."

Toby, failing to notice the amused smile, watched

him nod, walk toward the hatch, then disappear below. He turned to Harry Bailey. "How are you feeling now, Harry?"

"Pretty good, but I've never been so cold in my life, Toby."

"Well, you're better than halfway through your trick. It's warm down in the forecastle, and it won't be too long before you're down there. Think about that. Maybe it'll warm you up a little."

Harry nodded and said nothing. Toby moved forward very carefully on the slippery deck to work on the snow-covered running gear. He understood how the skipper felt. A frozen block at a critical time could be an expensive monument to carelessness, and John Talbott was not a careless man. He sailed his boat with skill and knowledge, relying on careful planning and long experience, leaving nothing to chance.

When someone spoke of mishaps narrowly missed and praised his luck, John Talbott snorted and said there was no such thing as luck, that the man had just planned better and more carefully than he realized, or else he had reacted faster; that every time a man went to sea there were risks, but that careful planning and experience reduced these risks to a bare minimum. This was one of the reasons he had

sailed that night with an experienced and devoted crew. There were few captains who were held in as high regard by their men. The rugged weather made it difficult enough to get good men for winter sailing, but add to that the slightest doubt of the skipper's seamanship, and his boat stayed in port.

In large measure this devotion of his men was the result of the devotion of the men who had sailed with him over the years. Their confidence in him had produced a confidence in himself. Their trust in him had produced a self-reliance and sureness that had fused into his personality. Thus he had come to believe, and with good reason, that no matter what trials might beset him, with careful planning he could master them.

Talbott was below for fifteen minutes. When he came back on deck Toby was working with a heavy broom and a hatchet around the main traveler across the stern aft of the wheel. One of the big wooden blocks for the mainsheet line made fast there and the snow had piled up worse than in most other places. If everything froze there they would not be able to trim the sails. The boy noticed that the skipper had put on dry clothing and another suit of oilskins, and was smoking a fresh cigar. He checked the compass and nodded. "Harry's watch is almost up, Toby. Go forward and tell Bull to get ready to relieve the wheel. Tell him to put on all the warm clothing he's got."

Toby eased his way forward, fighting every inch of the way to keep from slipping and falling on the deck. He knew that if he did he would slide all the way to the lee railing, and then maybe he'd stop himself and maybe he wouldn't.

He opened the doors to the forecastle, swung himself through, and climbed halfway down the ladder. He stopped short at the scene in the forecastle. "What's the matter down there, Bull?" he yelled, his voice high-pitched in horror.

Ed Shorter was on his hands and knees, crawling across the deck toward his bunk. He looked up with glassy eyes. His face was ashen and his jaw hung slack. As Toby's eyes took in the scene, his nose also took in the foul smell of the forecastle. He began to comprehend what had happened.

He watched Ed try to speak, then shut his mouth tightly. Toby watched his cheeks puff out until it seemed they would explode. Then suddenly it was as though they had. Toby leaped down the last three rungs of the ladder. He straddled Bull and hooked his hands under his stomach, lifting with each convulsion in an attempt to ease his struggle.

41

When the vomiting ceased he tried to heave him up off the floor and wrestle him into his bunk. It was all the boy could do to move the big man, and he almost lost his footing several times on the slimy deck before he managed to get him over near the bunk and spread him out on a clean spot. He pulled off the sick man's sea boots, stripped off his wet oilskins, pulled down the blankets on the bunk, and heaved and lifted and shoved until he got the limp body under the covers and the blankets tucked up around his neck.

Ed opened his eyes and stared blankly at Toby. He tried to smile and show how glad he was to see him, but somehow he just couldn't manage it. It seemed he had been alone so long, unable to call for help. He had been lying on his bunk for quite some time before he would admit to himself that something was wrong. He had been looking up at the lantern swinging from the middle of the forecastle ceiling. Its very motion seemed to disturb him, to aggravate the strange feelings he was experiencing in his stomach. The air in the forecastle was hot and stuffy. The coal stove had been allowed to get out of hand, he thought, noticing that the damper at the bottom was open. He slid off his bunk and staggered over and closed it, then opened the upper door. Once on his feet he realized the motion of the boat was not the only thing causing him to be unsteady. He turned and lurched back to his bunk. He looked straight up at the ceiling above him, carefully avoiding the swinging lantern. "I'm not seasick," he said aloud. "I never been seasick in my whole life. My insides are sure settin' in for a storm though. I feel like I'm gonna puke all over the place. Maybe I can make it to the deck and get some fresh air."

He rolled off the bunk and tried to stand, but just as he did the *Albatross* lurched and skittered and he went to his hands and knees. That same moment a violent wave of nausea hit him. It was uncontrollable. An explosion came bursting up through his throat. He tried to throttle it, but it continued to come surging up and when it found his teeth clenched and his lips tightly closed, it flooded into the back of his nasal passages and pushed on until it was running from his nostrils, forcing him to open his mouth. At the same time he felt the beginnings of a dizziness he had never known before, heard a keen whining noise in his ears, and felt himself beginning to move in great looping circles, until it all suddenly ceased and he knew nothing.

When consciousness returned he was in his bunk with Toby bending over him. "Never been seasick before," he mumbled. "Never."

Toby looked at the mess on the deck. The smell was almost more than he could stand. He tried to remember what Laura Talbott had done for him the last time he had been sick. The pounding and crashing of the *Albatross* made it hard to think.

He got the tin cup hanging by the forecastle water tank, filled it, and let Ed Shorter rinse out his mouth, spitting into the draw bucket that had been stowed under the ladder. He took a towel, wet it, and washed Ed's face. He couldn't think of anything else to do for the sick man, so he set out to try to clean the cabin. No one had a chance to recover with having to breathe the foul smell.

He took the draw bucket on deck, dropped it over the side to rinse it, pulled it back aboard, emptied it, and dropped it over again. He took the clean bucketful of seawater below, picked up the mop stowed under the ladder, and began to swab the deck. When he had finished he went up again, dumped the filthy contents over the side, and returned with a bucket of clean water to rinse with.

When he had finished he returned to Ed's bunk. "I'm going for the skipper," he said. "He'll probably have some medicine that will help."

Toby left the forecastle, leaving the hatch slightly open to allow fresh air to enter, and worked his way aft toward the wheel. It wasn't until he came around the corner of the aft cabin that he began to realize the full meaning of the message he was about to deliver. Without Bull, there were only the two of them to stand watch—only the three of them instead of four to handle the boat.

As he approached the wheel he heard the skipper holler, "Where's Bull?"

"He's in the fo'c'sle sick!"

"Sick? He can't be!"

"He's sicker'n anybody you ever saw," Toby shouted.

"What's the matter with him?"

"Says he's seasick."

"Ed Shorter seasick? Not a chance," the skipper shouted. "It's gotta be more than that."

"I know what's wrong with him," Harry Bailey shouted.

They both turned and looked at him.

"When I went up to his house to tell him we were going to sail, his wife was out at some church meeting or something and he said why didn't we go out and get some dinner?"

Suddenly Toby remembered the way Harry had acted in the galley less than an hour before. The memory of his flushed face and his remarks about feeling strange came back to the boy.

"So we went to a tavern not far from where he lives and we had oysters. Maybe they were spoiled. They didn't taste real good, but they didn't taste spoiled."

"I'll bet they were though," John Talbott shouted. "They don't have to be spoiled much to do that to you. I said earlier I didn't think there was a fresh oyster left in Baltimore and I reckon I was right." He paused, looking at Harry intently. "I reckon if you know what they tasted like you must have eaten them too."

"Yes, sir," Harry said, "and I've felt kinda funny for the last hour."

Chapter Four

"I'M GOING FORWARD, Toby!" the skipper shouted. "But first I'll see what I've got in the medicine chest below. You two stay up here in the fresh air." He disappeared into the aft cabin.

As he entered his own cabin he looked at the clock over the chart table. It said 2:04. Harry's watch was up and there was no one to relieve him except the boy and if he was relieved he certainly shouldn't come in out of the fresh air. He'd be sick for certain. But the time on the clock was more important than that. For the first time since he had heard about the sick man he stopped to make a choice. The hour had passed without his noting a position in the log and on the chart. That should be done, since he knew it might be the last one he would make in hours. He had to know where he was, or at least where his dead reckoning showed him to be, and the more current the position the better. If he lost the *Hattie* in the snow it would be the only thing he had to go on.

But Bull needed attention. He looked at the medicine cabinet on the bulkhead. He looked at the chart table and again at the clock. He had wasted one precious minute trying to make a decision.

He took a deep breath and walked to the chart table. This had to be done, he thought, but he knew it wouldn't take long and could be very important.

He took his parallel rule and pencil and began to mark off his course. Then he took the dividers and spread them along the closest meridian. He measured off the proper number of minutes of latitude, each minute representing a nautical mile, then moved the dividers over to the course line he had drawn, put one point on the last estimated position, and stuck the other point through the paper farther along the line. He took the pencil and marked an "X" over the dot on the chart. He wrote "2 A.M." alongside it.

His eyes swept the area around the "X," taking in the points of land and where they lay, the shoals and markers, and it was almost as if he were on deck on a clear day looking out over the water. If he was where his dead reckoning showed him to be, then he was completely familiar with his surroundings and knew exactly how they would look if he could see them.

He snapped the dividers closed, picked up the rule and the pencil, tossed them all in the drawer and closed it. He turned and opened the medicine chest. He puffed on his extinguished cigar as he examined the contents. Then he reached up and pulled down a package of Dover's Powder. Things would get a lot worse before they got any better, but if there was anything left in Bull's stomach this would get it out, and it would sweat some of it out too. There was nothing else that looked as if it might do the job. He was not exactly prepared for this type of illness. He was more prepared for cuts and bruises. He shook out a half dozen of the small paper envelopes of powder and put them on the chart table.

As he came down the forecastle ladder he saw that Ed Shorter was awake. He watched as the man shifted his eyes and slowly turned his head when

Talbott approached the bunk. "Never been seasick before," he said weakly.

"You're not seasick. Those oysters were spoiled."

"Harry ate 'em too," Ed said weakly.

"I know," the skipper said. He drew a fresh cup of water from the forecastle tank, dissolved three of the powders in the water, and said, "Open your mouth."

When he had finished, the skipper said, "Now you stay in that bunk. You're no good to me the way you are right now. But if you'll stay there for a while you might be. And I don't need you right now, but I'm sure going to need you later."

"Yes, sir," Ed said meekly. He didn't feel like moving at all. He thought about Harry and wondered if he would get sick. He wondered if the skipper and Toby could handle the boat by themselves. He wondered if the crew would be alive in the morning. He had never thought about dying before, but he thought about it now.

Up on deck Toby had watched the skipper leave for the forecastle with the medicine and knew he was going to be out of calling range if something went wrong. He glanced at the light on the *Hattie* and felt that it seemed to be a bit farther ahead than it had been before. He wondered what he should do. It was one thing to do what the skipper said, but here he was, responsible for the boat, and it seemed that he'd have to make a decision. Suddenly he understood the reason the skipper sometimes seemed lost in thought. "We're losing her, Harry."

"I know! We're falling behind. What should we do?"

He had hoped that Harry, who was seven years older, might have some idea, but now he knew Harry didn't know what to do either. He wished John Talbott would hurry. The *Hattie* would soon be out of sight. He looked back over the stern at the seas piling up behind them, their tops reflected in the lantern's light. And suddenly he knew what was wrong. "Wind is working around!" he shouted. "Sheets need easing again!"

He quickly worked his way forward across the icy deck to where the jib sheet was cleated to the deck. He eased it gently until he caught the first flutter, then took it in a little and made fast.

He was just turning from the deck cleat where he had eased the mainsail when the boat yawed violently. She was going around into the troughs of the waves. He turned, a shout dying in his throat. Harry was on his hands and knees, vomiting on the deck. The wheel was free. He started for it, slipped, fell to the deck, got up and threw himself toward the wheel. This time he made it. He grabbed the spokes and swung the plunging boat back on her course.

During the entire time it seemed he never took his eyes off the lantern on the stern of the *Hattie*. Even when he slipped on the deck he was still looking at it. He kept it in sight and as he eased the helm back amidships and let the *Albatross* settle back on her course he could still see it, a diffuse glow out there in the snow. It was the only thing he could see that was a part of the *Hattie*. No detail of her hull, her rigging, or even her yawl davits, was visible— just the light.

Suddenly he looked around for Harry. He was not on the deck by the wheel anymore. His eyes swept the deck and then he saw him, crumpled up in a ball over by the starboard railing. He had been swept across the deck as the boat yawed to port. The bow plunged into a wave, and the stern rose out of the water. Harry slid forward along the rail, almost to the point where he was hidden by the aft cabin trunk. The bow came up, the boat shuddered, and Harry slid aft, almost to the big main traveler. He reached out, grabbed a deck cleat, and held on.

Toby held the wheel and watched Harry slide, powerless to help him. The bow plunged again and

Harry slid forward again, not able to hold onto the slippery deck cleat. With the next wave he slid aft again. This time he was able to wrap both arms around the cleat and when the next wave passed them he was still there.

For several minutes the boat seemed to ride smoothly, and during this time Harry left the cleat and crawled slowly toward the aft companionway. Just before he got there the next wave arrived, the bow went down as the stern came up, and Harry was sliding forward again. But this time he slid only as far as the cabin bulkhead. He reached out his hand and grabbed for the ledge at the top of the ladder going down into the cabin. The bow came up, but he was able to hold on and stay where he was.

He put one leg over the ledge and down onto the ladder, then the other. He sat there for a moment, holding onto the doorjamb on each side. Toby watched him and wondered whether he would be able to get down the ladder safely.

"Harry," he shouted. "Harry! Harry!"

Harry turned his head slowly and looked up at him. His eyes were glazed and his mouth hung open. Toby was reminded of Bull Shorter in the forecastle. It was difficult to believe Harry knew what was happening. "Go in the skipper's cabin. I'll send him down as soon as he gets back."

Harry nodded vaguely. He turned, got his tail up over the ledge, and slid down the ladder. Toby watched him vanish, watched his hands slide from around the doorjambs, and then saw nothing more of him. He could not see down into the cabin from where he was standing. He had no way of knowing how Harry had fallen, or if he had fallen at all. Suddenly he saw a small amount of light through the companionway and knew that he had opened the door to the skipper's cabin. So far, so good. He returned his attention to the boat. There was nothing else he could do but wait until the skipper got back from the forecastle.

Snow was still sticking to everything. The entire boat had become a ghostly white web of spars and rigging. She plunged and shuddered and pitched and yawed. She was a wild, scared, female thing, going in all directions, challenging his strength and skill to anticipate what she might do next.

He was alone—a solitary figure on the deck of a ninety-foot schooner, a fourteen-year-old boy alone and already weary from the efforts of the last hour. Alone and unable to move, he was bound to the wheel just as surely as if he were actually wrapped in chains and padlocked to the wheelbox. He was alone, unable to do anything except follow the light on the *Hattie*. Regardless of what was happening, regardless of its effect on the *Albatross,* he could not leave the wheel until the skipper returned from the forecastle.

He looked around at the harsh unfriendliness of the now unfamiliar surroundings. The lantern hanging in the yawl davits was bright and its light was reflected by the snow and ice, giving even more light to the distressing scene around him, forcing him to look at what was happening. He wished the skipper would hurry.

He was reminded of the times his mother had taken him to visit at her parents' home in the country and put him to bed all alone in the little room in the attic. The house was quiet and he couldn't hear the grown-ups talking downstairs. He could hear the creaking of the rafters, and the lamp his mother left at the head of the stairs threw those deep shadows around the room. He felt awfully small and alone, saw things back in the corners, heard noises and didn't know what they were. He would have got out of bed and gone downstairs if he hadn't been too scared to move.

Looking out across the *Albatross,* he saw nothing

that reminded him of the soft beauty of the snow he had seen as they left home, the snow piled on the trees and bushes around the house, reflected in the gentle glow of the flickering gas lamp on the street corner. Now he saw a deck harshly white with snow until a wave washed over the stern and swept the snow away, revealing patches of harsh glare ice, hard and slippery. There were no soft edges or gently rounded corners, only sharp edges of ice where the wind had blown the snow away. The rigging was coated with ice—shiny, ragged ice, pockmarked and evil-looking. His ears were assailed by the rushing, booming, and the roar of the wind. When he looked around at the following sea he saw waves rise above the stern, saw the tops blow off into a fine mist, and felt the hard, frigid drops of water hit his face like icy needlepoints. He wished the skipper would hurry.

He almost shouted for joy when he saw a shadow materialize in the doorway to the forecastle, saw the shadow become a person, and saw the person become John Talbott when he stepped around the aft cabin trunk into the light from the lantern in the yawl davits.

"Where's Harry?" he shouted.

Toby pointed down the companionway and the

skipper vanished again. The boy was alone again. All that he saw was stark, harsh, and threatening, and he knew he was getting colder and colder and colder. He thought of the times he had gone sledding, walked a long way to find a good hill, and then coasted all afternoon until the time came to start home for dinner. It was always the same. You thought you'd never get there because you were so cold. Your feet felt like blocks of ice and you couldn't wait to get to the bathroom. You kept walking and the sun went down and you could see the house, but it seemed as if you weren't getting any closer.

He wondered how long he could stand it. He knew it would make a difference if he could move around a little. Go below and get a cup of coffee. Just walk around and move his muscles. Suppose something had happened to the skipper. Suppose he had fallen and hurt himself and wouldn't be coming back on deck. Suppose Toby had to sail the boat all night long. He could hardly think about that —he was too cold. But he knew that if he had to do that he hadn't really *begun* to get cold yet. If he had to do that it would get bad, really bad. In an hour he would really be cold. What could be keeping the skipper? Why didn't he come?

The snow was getting deeper. He thought about the snow piled up around that nice warm house back in Baltimore. He thought about his classmates in their warm beds. He thought of how his mother had constantly complained about his father's never being home, always being out on some boat going somewhere. He could hardly remember his father. He had never seen very much of him—always off on a boat somewhere. And now Toby was off on a boat somewhere. His mother would have hated that. But he was steering the boat, sailing her, something his father had never done. And he was going to be a captain someday and own his own boat, something his father had never done. And he was never going to be lost at sea. He would hold that wheel until the skipper returned and he would follow that light out there in the snow all night if he had to. If he did these things he would survive and someday he would be a captain and own his own boat and make his mother proud of him.

He turned and saw her standing on the deck beside him, a look of fury on her face. She was standing in the snow, but there was no snow on her coat and no snow on the shawl that covered her head. She looked at him but did not speak.

He spoke to her: "I won't be lost at sea. I'll own

a boat like this someday. I'll be a captain and I'll make you proud of me someday."

She shook her head and said nothing, the look of anger still on her face.

"Not all sailors are like what you thought he was," he said. "The skipper is a good man and some-day . . ."

She did not move. She stood in the snow and stared at him but did not move. The expression of anger changed to pity and she seemed to be crying. And then she was gone.

The light on the *Hattie* rose and fell in the sea-way. His eyes followed it with a vacant, uncomprehending stare.

Toby Wheeler never remembered the skipper's shouting at him when he returned to the deck; he never remembered the brandy forced between his lips, never remembered stumbling down the ladder into the aft cabin; but as long as he lived he would remember the feeling of complete surrender as he fell across his bunk and knew his fight was over.

Chapter Five

JOHN TALBOTT watched Toby stumble down into the aft cabin, saw the glow through the open hatch, and knew he had found his way to his cabin. He was appalled to see what less than an hour out in the weather at the wheel had done to the boy. But he was proud of him, proud of the way he had taken care of Bull, proud of the way he had taken command of the boat, proud of the way he had stood fast at the wheel and followed the light even though the weather was overwhelming him.

He needed to know what time it was and he

couldn't see the clock. He had to know the time so he'd know where he was. He had to keep track of it. That was all he had now. There was snow all over the binnacle—snow all over everything. He brushed off the binnacle, then he could see the clock. It was 2:48. Forty-eight minutes since. . . . He had to stop and think for a minute. So much had happened since he had marked that "X" on the chart. Then he remembered. Just off Thomas Point. That was right. He had figured that in an hour and twelve minutes from now he would be off the mouth of Herring Bay. South end, probably.

He knew he'd never find it. Have to jibe anyway. No sense even thinking about it. He knew he'd never make it—not without another man on deck. He didn't even know for sure where he was. The only thing he could do now was hope. Hope that Tom Webster knew where *he* was. He couldn't lose him now. He had to stay with him.

He guessed in twenty more minutes he'd be off Black Walnut Point. He wouldn't have to jibe to get into there. But he'd have to lay her broadside to the wind and he couldn't trim her sails. Might miss the mouth of the Choptank and wind up ashore.

Oysters! Oysters! Cursed oysters! I don't ever want to see another oyster as long as I live. Maybe

I won't have the chance. Made my men sick, made me come out here tonight when any man in his right mind would be home in bed. God, it's cold! Home in bed. Can't think of that now. It's warm there. I can't think about that. Only makes it seem worse.

He wondered why he had done this. She had asked him not to. She had told him they didn't need the money. And he knew that was true. He could have been warm in bed and asleep by now. He knew he had to stop thinking about that.

He tried to be honest about it. He knew he had wanted to come. He really had wanted to. He knew it wasn't the money at all. That was only an excuse. His friends and some of his relatives needed coal, but that was only part of the reason. Mainly he wanted to go. Things had been all right until the men got sick. They would have made out fine. They would have been in Solomons when the sun came up. And the sun would be coming up in the morning, he was sure of that.

He hadn't noticed the cold before the men got sick. It was so easy to find all sorts of things that were wrong now. It always was that way when things weren't going exactly as they should.

He concentrated on the time: five-thirty, six o'clock at the latest. That's when they would have reached Solomons. Three more hours. If he had a crew. *If I only had a crew. What the hell, she might break up by then. I'm driving her too hard, but there's nothing I can do about it. I'm carrying too much sail. But I can't shorten sail. I'd need a crew and I haven't got a crew. I shouldn't even be out here.*

He hadn't thought he was carrying too much sail when he left Baltimore. He had had her reefed down and had come out without the foresail. It seemed to make sense then. He hadn't felt he was carrying too much sail that first hour after they turned down the Bay.

He knew he could do without the mainsail. He could sail her all night long with just the jib up there pulling her along. Of course, he wouldn't be able to stay with the *Hattie.* He wouldn't be able to do that much longer anyway. He would lose her off the mouth of the Patuxent. He didn't have a crew to handle the mainsail and jib when the time came to jibe. With the wind dead astern and blowing a gale the mainsail and boom would whip across the deck with unbelievable force. It was nothing like bringing the bow of the boat into the wind and going about. Running before the wind as they were, the mainsail was at almost a ninety-degree angle to the boat. If it swung one hundred and eighty degrees with all that wind behind it it would carry away the mast and God only knew what else. It needed a man to lower the main peak, then gentle the main boom in as close to straight fore and aft as possible, then a slight change in course to fill the sail on the other side and ease it out again. It was a highly delicate maneuver. He doubted if Toby could do it, wasn't sure about Harry, but knew Bull could handle it easily. But he didn't think any of them would be able to lend a hand in three hours.

Off the mouth of the Patuxent, Tom Webster would jibe and go into the river, and Talbott would be left powerless to follow. He would have to sail all night long, if he could stand on his feet and his boat held together.

Damn Tom Webster and his luck! He talks about it all the time and I can see why he does. He wouldn't have been out here tonight if I hadn't gotten him to thinking about it, and here he is, sailing down the Bay like all hell's after him, and pretty soon he won't have any competition getting those oysters back to Baltimore because even if we're lucky enough to live through this we'll be so far down the Bay we won't get home before Easter.

He looked up at the snow. He was worried about

the blocks in the upper rigging. He was afraid they were frozen. He thought about the time again. He brushed off the binnacle so he could see the clock. Three-thirty. Two and a half more hours. At six o'clock Tom Webster and his crew would be in Solomons and he would be lost on the Bay.

If he had a crew he could get his crew to a doctor in Solomons. If he had a crew he could get them into a harbor and anchor until they got well. "What the hell!" he shouted. She might break up by then. God, she's pounding.

"Old girl, I'm glad they built you right," he shouted into the wind, hardly aware he was speaking aloud. "I'm glad somebody took the time and the trouble to put you together well. I'm glad the men who worked on you knew what they were doing and gave a damn about their work. It don't seem like there are many like that around anymore. I hope you'll hold together. I know you'll do your part to get me through this night. I hope I can do my part to get you through it. I'll bet it'll take more than this to pull you apart, won't it, old girl? You aren't going to come apart on me, are you? It isn't even bothering you, is it? You must wonder what the hell I'm trying to do to you though, don't you? Well, old girl, I don't know how I could have been

fool enough to have gotten us into this mess tonight."

It was greed, that's what it was, he thought. And
then he decided he didn't think it was greedy of him
to come out. He was giving himself hell again just
because things weren't going right. He was feeling
sorry for himself for what had happened. It was a
hard life. This was part of it. They'd make it.

He wondered how long he could stand it. He
knew it would make a difference if he could move
around a little. Go below and get a cup of coffee.
Just walk around and move his muscles. He was so
cold, but he knew he wasn't cold compared to what
was coming.

The *Albatross* was beginning to gripe a little. He
could feel the rudder pulling on the wheel and the
wheel pulling on his hands. He wondered what the
wind was going to do. He wished he could ease the
mainsheet a little. He knew the wind was backing
around more and more and knew she should have
been running freer than she was.

The snow was getting deeper. He thought about
the snow piled up around his home. He wondered if
Laura was asleep. He needed to know the time and
brushed off the binnacle again. Quarter to four. He
caught a glimpse of the compass. *By God, look at*

that compass. He's heading right for the barn all right. He's got us aimed in the right direction, that's certain.

My God! That was a wave! Almost lost her that time. She was starting to slide around for certain. Thank God they aren't all like that one. Got him too. Now he's got her back. I think I'm closing up on him a little. He looks a little closer than he was awhile ago. I certainly don't want to pass him.

He had to do something about the mainsheet though. It was getting very hard to hold her. He wondered if he could reach the line without letting go the wheel. He tried and lacked a foot. He thought about lashing the wheel down for a moment. That was all it would take. He took a loop around a spoke and pulled it tight around a cleat. He turned and freed the mainsheet. He eased her and she sailed better.

Sure is snowing all right. Flakes are getting bigger though. That's supposed to mean it's going to stop soon. He brushed off the binnacle again. Ten after four. He had been there at the wheel for over an hour. Not a soul on deck but him. No one to talk to. No one to relieve him. He remembered four-hour tricks at the wheel that had gone by on wings. He had been there only a little more than an hour and already his legs ached and his back, in the middle, over his kidneys, was an agony to him. He knew the snow matted to the back of his coat must be an inch thick. And he knew there were hours more of this to come. He couldn't give up. They were counting on him. Bull, Harry, and Toby. If he couldn't keep the boat on the right course they would all die. He would too.

Laura was counting on him too. But she wouldn't die if he failed. It wasn't the same as with the crew. But she was counting on him. The children wouldn't die either, but they were counting on him and didn't even know it. Christmas was coming. What a poor Christmas they would have if . . .

It seems like all my life someone's been counting on me for something. Crew, they always count on the skipper. Once they're aboard and the boat leaves the slip it's total dependence. I could be a rotten skipper and they'd have to do what I said.

People I've never seen have been counting on me too. Farmers sending their year's work to market. They've counted on me to carry it safely for them. I've carried their corn, their cantaloupes, their oysters, their hogs. I'll never carry any damn hogs again. That was a mess.

And I've brought them things. They've depended

on me to get their coal to them, their coal oil, lots of things. And I've always done it. That's what I'm doing tonight—trying to get some coal to those people down around Solomons. I'll bet some of them are pretty nearly out.

He could have stayed in port. He could have dipped into that savings account. But he had never touched it. But he could have. He would have, maybe, but those people needed that coal. He remembered the day that savings account started. Laura's father had given them a twenty-dollar gold piece on their wedding day. Told them it was for the children's college education.

She was a lovely bride—so beautiful. Everybody said so. Everybody always says that about a bride, but I thought she was and that's all that mattered. It was like I hadn't ever seen her before. When I looked down the aisle and saw her coming toward me with her father, she was beautiful. I hope Toby finds someone like her someday.

He wondered what Tom Webster was doing. He seemed to be changing course, but only a little and away from the shore and that was all right. It took a little of the gripe off the rudder. Made it easier for him to steer. He wondered what would happen if he tied the wheel down and ran below for a cup of coffee or a swallow of that brandy. He wouldn't drink it down, just grab it and run back up on deck. He could do it in less than a minute.

I must be out of my mind thinking I could do something like that. If I moved fast maybe I could though. I think I'll tie her down and see how she sails for a couple of minutes. Got to shake the snow off this line. It's frozen again. Sure is stiff. So am I. Stiff. My back aches like hell too. Feels like I've been lifting something heavy all day long. But it never gets sore when I lift. Not ever. But it sure is sore right now. Right down in the small of it.

He got the rope lashed to the spoke and took his hands off the wheel to see how she would do. But she wouldn't hold course. Every time a wave hit her from behind she sheered off to windward. He could tell it wouldn't work.

He could remember the first time he saw Laura. She was sitting on the wharf at Point Patience, waiting for the steamer, all dressed up to go to Baltimore with her mother and father. He had just finished loading a crop of tobacco. Stole it right out from under the steamer. The steamer was coming down the river past Hawk's Nest buoy when they finished. He made up his mind he would have to find some way to meet her. He didn't know who she was and she hadn't paid any attention to him; he certainly didn't blame her for that. He wasn't much to look at that day—not for a pretty girl like her. He was dirty and sweaty from trying to get the cargo aboard before the steamer got there. Bad enough to steal her cargo without holding her off the wharf while they finished loading.

Old Doc Parrish was standing there watching us load, he thought. It was his cotton. It wasn't cotton; it was tobacco. Never loaded any cotton.

But it was his tobacco. That's what it was—tobacco. I asked him who she was. He kinda smiled and said she was his niece and wouldn't I like to meet her and I knocked ten dollars off his shipping charges right on the spot. He took me over and introduced me. I remember how polite she was, so pleased to meet me and all that. Said she was surprised I was the captain of such a big boat. Said she didn't think the captain would be working with the deckhands to load the boat.

But she got a real devilish little gleam in her eye when I told her why we were in such a hurry. She laughed at that and said I must be a pretty good talker if I got a cargo away from the steamer seeing as how Doctor Parrish had a nephew on her.

I can still remember the way he laughed and said

he knew her brother was mate on the steamboat, but business was business and I was a pretty good talker all right, but money was the best talker and I was hauling his cotton cheaper than he could send it on the steamer.

We got away from there just as the steamboat was blowing for the landing and we got a pretty nice slant of wind coming out of the mouth of the river and were almost up to Chesapeake Beach when she came up abeam of us on the starboard side. Laura was standing at the bow rail on the top deck as they went by, and she waved at me. She waved at me. Big floppy hat on her head, tied around under her chin, and she waved—and waved. With a big floppy hat on her head. My Laura. She waved.

It was warm that day. Not like tonight. Cold tonight. It was warm that day and the sun was shining and there was a sparkle on the water and the spray was white and the sails were white and there were puffy white clouds, and she waved and she was wearing a big white floppy hat and we were hauling white cotton up the Bay to Baltimore.

And everything's white now. Deck's white and the rigging's white and the sky's white and the masts are white and everything's white and Laura's not waving at me tonight.

*She's rolling too much and I've got to fight to keep
her on course. And I'm so sleepy. I've got to do
something to stay awake. Maybe I could count the
reef points on the mainsail. No point in that. Already
know how many there are. Thirty-one. At least I'd
know if I counted them right.*

*I guess I could sing. Not much of a singer, but it
might help keep me awake. Nobody around to hear
me, so I reckon it would be all right. Maybe it would
keep me awake. Wouldn't seem so lonesome either.
Be like whistling past the graveyard. What should
I sing, though?*

Toby Wheeler stirred slightly in his sleep. He was
dreaming of a warm Sunday morning in church. A
man was singing a familiar hymn:

"Eternal Father, strong to save,
Whose arm doth bind the restless wave . . ."

The sun was streaming through the stained-glass
windows; he could hear the birds singing in the trees
outside, the bees droning in the roses just under the
windows, the gentle rustle of cardboard fans. The
man was singing in a rich baritone voice:

"Who bidd'st the mighty ocean deep
Its own appointed limits keep . . ."

He listened and recognized the voice as that of
the skipper, but try as he would he could not see

him. The warmth and good feeling were over-whelming him with sleep and he could not manage to stay awake. He fought to hold his head up and keep his eyes open.

> *"O, hear us when we cry to Thee*
> *For those in peril on the sea!"*

Try as he would he could not stay awake. The church faded from his vision as he slipped back down into his deep sleep.

Chapter Six

Jᴏʜɴ ᴛᴀʟʙᴏᴛᴛ hoped none of the crew heard him singing that song. He didn't think there was much chance with the wind blowing the way it was and the state they were in. And it did wake him up a little, so there was something to be said for it, even if it didn't do anything else.

The snowflakes were getting larger. Maybe it really was going to stop pretty soon. It was beginning to look as if he might be right. *Hold her! Hold her! Easy does it, old girl. Almost lost her that time. Serves me right for thinking thoughts like that. No room for optimism in something like this. Just take what comes along. Can't start hoping for more than what's reasonable. That's the road to sure trouble.*

The wind gusts were increasing. They hit with more force than before. He wondered what that meant. The seas seemed bigger and choppier, more confused. The tops were blowing off. The spray was striking the back of his oilskins and sounded like hail. It was becoming more difficult to hold her on course. He wondered if he could lash the wheel again and ease the mainsheet and then he remembered he had made it fast to the cleat near his foot. He reached down and eased her again. The rudder eased and took the pressure off the wheel. Just the effort of reaching down and breaking loose the ice that had covered the cleat where the sheet line was tied had tired him. He knew it. He could feel the increased burden of his weariness.

But we're still afloat, by God! That's something to be thankful for, considering the state of the men and that I'm alone. They wouldn't have much chance if I were to fall apart, but as long as I can stay awake and we can stay afloat, we'll just have to thank God for that small benefit. And every hour brings us closer to the dawn. Now that's a lovely sentence: "Every hour brings us closer to the dawn." I don't reckon there'll be much of a dawn though. But at least it will be light and I can see.

He didn't like the way the mast was bending. Sail only a little more than halfway up with a double reef and still the mast was bowed. He had never driven her like this before and hoped he never would again. He wished he knew what was happening to the men. If only he had one of them to relieve him he could take a moment and get something warm in his stomach.

Wonder if I can light a cigar in this damn gale of wind. Got one here someplace, if it's not soaking wet or crushed. Here it is. Feels all right. Now if the match will only light. Clumsy work, cold fingers, damn near numb. Damn! Went out before I even got it to the cigar. Try again. A little longer. Please burn a little longer this time. Got it! Oh, that tastes good. That's a damn fine cigar. Wish I had a nice hot toddy to go along with it.

Wish I were sitting at home in front of the fire with this cigar and a hot toddy. That would be nice.

He needed to know the time again. He brushed away the snow. It had got to be an awful effort to get the binnacle clear. Ten until five. It wouldn't be long now. No more than an hour, but how would they know it for sure? If they were close enough to see the light at Cove Point in this snow they would go aground for sure. The *Hattie* was less than twenty yards away and he doubted if he could have even made out her light had she been much farther away. If it hadn't been for the lantern in her yawl davits he wouldn't have been able to see her at all.

The *Albatross* was getting harder to steer again. She just wouldn't stay on course. He talked to her, cajoled her, and begged her to sail a straight course. And then he began to talk to Tom Webster and tell him to sail a straight course. He knew it wasn't the *Albatross* that was wandering all over the Bay. Tom Webster must be having his troubles too. That was why he was not sailing a straight course. "It isn't the old *Albatross,* I know that. This old girl knows the course. She could almost do it on her own, as many times as she's made this run. But you've never made it in this kind of a blow, have you? Don't worry, old girl," he said aloud. "We'll find us a home somewhere. We'll find a place to land this coal somewhere. As soon as the daylight comes we'll get into someplace and make a record turnaround and beat that old buzzard back to Baltimore. We can do it. We'll come sailing up that channel and be the first ones, the very first ones. We can do it, old girl, you and I.

"I wish the boys could be here to see this. I should take them with me a little more often than I have. Doesn't seem like I take them sailing at all except when they go down to visit their grandparents and God Almighty they don't understand why we don't send them down on the damn steamboat. Where's the steamboat tonight? Ha! Tied up at the dock in Baltimore, that's where she is tonight!"

He decided he would take them all sailing one day in the spring—when the weather warmed up and looked as if it would stay good for a few days. Maybe he'd take them down to Point Lookout to see the monument with his father's name on it. He thought of his father and wished he could have known him, even for a little while. Three years in that prison camp and then he died two weeks before the war ended. He must have known nights like this when he was there, living out in the open—cold, hungry, sick. Poor man.

But he would take the boys sailing. Let them sleep in the forecastle with Bull and Harry. They'd like that. He had never done that and couldn't figure out why. *You'd enjoy that, wouldn't you, Jack?*

He looked around. The snow was gone and the sun was out. The day was warm and clear. The boy stood beside him looking up at him.

"What's that place over there? Why, that's Point Patience, son. No, I don't know why they call it Point Patience. Maybe because some fisherman wasted a lot of time there and didn't catch any fish."

"Those things? They're whirlpools, Dickey-boy. The water is very deep around the point and the river is narrow here."

"How deep is it? One hundred and twenty feet in some places."

"How deep is that? Well, it's twice as high as that mast. That's how deep it is."

"Come back here, Dickey-boy. Where are you going?"

"To the top of the mast! You can't go up there. It's cold up there and you might slip and fall. Do you see that wharf over there? Well, that's where I met your mother. She was sitting there waiting for the steamboat and I was taking on a big load of tobacco. And do you know something, she got on the steamboat and I followed the steamboat all night long in the old *Albatross.* Followed the light on the steamboat in the snow and it was so cold—" *Why is he turning again? He must be having trouble over there. I keep having to change course all the time to stay with him. He keeps wandering off from one side to the other. God, it's snowing so hard all of a sudden. I must have drifted off again. I must have been dreaming. I've got to stay awake. But he's having trouble with those waves hitting her in the stern.*

They weren't giving him any trouble anymore. He was handling her much better than he had been an hour before. He knew that. He was glad the crew was below, where it was warm. He was enjoying himself up here all alone. Things were beginning to work out. Soon the snow would stop, the air would clear, and then they'd see Cove Point after all. And he could handle the main peak himself all right. Tie the helm down and lower the peak and then jibe and go into Solomons. He wasn't even cold anymore.

"OUCH!" He had let go the wheel, and the spokes had cracked his knuckles. *I must have been asleep again. What was I thinking about? I've got to stop this drifting off and thinking about lowering the main peak and jibing all by myself. What a fool I am! It would take two good men, maybe three, with that wind blowing and all that ice. I've got to stay awake.*

He had to stop pretending that things would work out as he had planned them. His mother had always told him to plan things. He could remember her saying there wasn't any such thing as luck—that you had to plan very carefully and if you did everything carefully that you planned, all would work out fine. Well, he had planned this very carefully and look what had happened. No such thing as luck? His mother should have talked to Tom Webster. He'd have told her about luck.

She had always said to have an alternative, just in case things didn't work out or something went wrong. Well, it had certainly gone wrong tonight. You could lay to that.

"I wish she could see me now. I wish she could see all of this. If she was proud of me the day the block froze at the masthead of that oyster canoe and I went up there and freed it she'd be prouder of me tonight. Here I am—I wish he'd stop that wandering —all alone on the deck of a ninety-foot schooner, my own ninety-foot schooner, carrying more sail than anybody's got a right to be carrying. It's a vicious battle with the weather. You fight it and you can't ever beat it. Eventually it stops fighting you, but you don't beat it. You never beat it. But at this point it's still a stalemate, and when you can't win, that's what you play for—a stalemate." He was talking out loud again.

He turned and spoke to his mother. She was standing beside him in the snow, but there was no snow on her cape and no snow in her hair. She stared at him but did not speak.

"Isn't she a beautiful boat, Mother? Look how she drives along. See how she plunges her bow into the wave and raises her stern on the top of the wave. She's been doing this for hours and she could do it for hours longer if she had to. Listen to the wind singing in the rigging as it blasts through, and feel the snow falling all around us on the deck.

"There's no need to be frightened, Mother. Things will calm in a little while. The men will be on the decks again soon and the snow will stop and the weather will clear and we'll see Cove Point Light shining out across the water and then we'll slip in around Drum Point and into the calm water beyond. She'll do it.

"I'm simply carrying out my plan, Mother. Why are you shaking your head? My plan was to come down the Bay tonight, following the light you put in the window for me to follow. The same light that has burned there every night. The light the steamers use to come into the creek. The lantern on the end of the wharf and the light in the window. Come down the river until the light in the window appears, turn toward it, stay on the course until you see the lantern on the end of the wharf. How many

times have I done that! And I can do it again tonight, in spite of this weather. Don't shake your
head, Mother.

"We're going home, Mother, going home, following the light in the window. Or is it the lantern on
the end of the wharf? It doesn't look like the light in
the window; it looks more like a lantern. I'm so cold
and confused I only know I have to follow it.

"NO!" he shouted. "That's the lantern on the stern
of the *Hattie*. And he's moving off course again.
Why can't he hold a steady course? I've got to stay
awake and follow him. I can't lose him. I've got to
follow that lantern or I'll run up on the point and
never make it to the wharf."

He looked at his mother helplessly. He was very
cold. He needed something warm to drink, something to take the chill off. He was trying to act like
a man and he wanted a man's drink. He needed a
big mug of hot buttered rum, that was what he
needed. He wished she'd take him out of the cold
and fix him a good hot mug and let him go to sleep.
As soon as they made the wharf they would go up
to the house and she would fix something for him
and she must have one too because he knew she was
cold.

He asked her to hold the wheel for him for a little

while. He asked her to let him sleep for a little while right there on the deck. He would wake up shortly and they would land at the wharf and go home and then they could sit under the maple trees in the front yard and have a hot toddy. "You can do it, Mother. You can do anything. All you have to do is follow that lantern. We can't lose Tom Webster or we'll never find our way. You can do it. Why won't you do it?"

He stared at her, but she did not move. She stood in the snow and looked back at him but did not move. And then she was gone. He shook his head bitterly and then stared at the light. *The boat can take care of herself for a few minutes if I get forty winks and then wake up. She knows the way. I'll just get forty winks and leave her to herself. And when I wake up the storm will be over and the air will be clear and the men will be well and we'll make the wharf and she will be waiting for me and she'll have something for me to drink and we'll sit under the trees in the front yard and that's where she went—she went to fix something warm for me to drink! That's where she went!*

The light on the *Hattie* rose and fell in the seaway. His eyes followed it with a vacant, uncomprehending stare.

87

Suddenly he was jolted awake! Something big was happening! He opened his eyes and saw Toby standing in front of him shouting, "Skipper! Skipper! SKIPPER! Wake up! We're going to JIBE!"

He shook his head violently and tried to focus his brain. The last stray, lingering, wandering thoughts of a green lawn, the shaded, blue-green grass under the maple trees, the white chairs on the lawn, the view of the river with a white sailboat lying motionless against the blue hills on the far shore—these last remaining thoughts were swept away by the pounding of the water, the rush and howl of the wind, the crashing of the bow as it plunged into a wave, and Toby's face, harsh and stark in the raw white light of the lantern still hanging in the yawl davits. His face was contorted and he was shouting. There was a rapping noise followed by an explosive roar. The jib suddenly collapsed and then burst forth on the port side with a resounding roar, sending a wild spray of splintered ice into the air. Very slowly the thought began to work its way around the edges of his brain and down into his understanding that Toby was telling him that they were about to jibe and he knew this was something they certainly should not do, but he was powerless at the moment to do anything that might prevent this.

Suddenly he felt the wheel move and realized he was still holding a spoke in each hand and that Toby had grabbed two other spokes and was spinning the wheel in a frantic attempt to hold the air in the rapping mainsail. The jib collapsed again like a balloon without air and burst out on the starboard side again. The danger of jibing seemed to be past.

He shook his head and stared wildly at Toby, trying to figure what had happened, and as the two stood facing each other with the wheel between them his brain began to clear. The wind, in its movement around to the northwest, had now crossed over his stern and was coming across the starboard quarter. It had reached the point where it had almost flipped the big sail and sent it crashing across the deck, which would have carried away the sail, the boom, the mast, and all of the rigging.

He was wide-awake now. He watched the light on the *Hattie* recede into the snow and knew he had no choice. The *Hattie* had jibed, she must have jibed, but she was fading into the snow fast and he knew he would never find her again. But he was alert again. Toby was on deck. Toby was there and now maybe there was hope. Perhaps the two of them could do what had seemed impossible. He wondered how Toby had happened to come on deck at that particular moment.

Toby had been deep in sleep one moment and wide-awake and leaping off his bunk the next. He had felt the change in the motion of the boat, nothing more, and it had brought him fully awake. Instead of the plowing into one wave after another, the bow rising, the stern lowering, the stern rising, the bow lowering, there was a persistent rapping and the *Albatross* began rocking from side to side like a skiff. Before his feet touched the deck he had analyzed the motion and knew it could mean only one thing: disaster. This type of motion preceded an uncontrolled jibe.

Now that the immediate disaster had been averted, both he and the skipper turned to watch the receding light of the *Hattie*. Both were surprised to see that the air was clearing rapidly. The light on the *Hattie* was no longer indistinct and diffuse. It was sharp and clear. Snow was still falling, big white flakes of it, and the wind was still blowing as hard as ever, but the visibility had improved and it was now possible to make out the red of the *Hattie*'s port running light as well as the light that had been visible all night long. Both knew that the sudden shift of wind heralded the end of the storm.

Then, for one brief instant, they saw two white lights, one above and in front of the other, and one red light, below and in between the white ones. Then the upper light was gone. And then it appeared again, but this time it appeared alone just as the two other lights suddenly vanished. And then, like the blasts of a double-barreled shotgun, two loud reports came downwind, ending in a splintering crash. At that instant the bottom of the *Albatross* hit sand, John Talbott was thrown against the wheel, Toby Wheeler was thrown against the cabin trunk, and the white lantern that had been in the yawl davits came crashing down onto the icy deck and went out.

Chapter Seven

A s JOHN TALBOTT fought to hold his footing on the slippery deck, and Toby Wheeler attempted to struggle to his feet using the cabin trunk as a hand-hold, they could feel the bottom of the *Albatross* scrape across the sand, push mightily for what seemed like hours, and then slide off into the deep again. And for the first time in hours the skipper knew exactly where he was. He knew he had just passed over Cove Point. Ahead lay the sheltering Cliffs of Calvert, and five miles away was Solomons Island, his destination. Five more miles and then safety, a doctor for his men, a snug harbor, and blessed sleep.

It took no great imagination to reconstruct what had happened. It had been such a swift change, such a rapid passage of events that he had not had time to reason them out as they were happening. He had been able to concentrate only on fighting against the wheel to keep from being thrown to the deck; his only thought had been bare survival and the fervent hope that his boat would push on, push herself into the clear again, and he had not really thought of what was happening and its cause. But now he had the time to think for a moment and consider the sudden turn of events that had put him where he was.

He knew that the *Hattie* had gone hard-and-fast ashore on the point, rather close to the lighthouse, he judged from the way he remembered the position of the lights. At the speed she was traveling he imagined she might have finally stopped with her hull pretty much out of the water, although he knew the surf would be pounding around her until the wind decreased. She was probably a total loss, her rigging shattered, her hull stove in, but he doubted that her cargo would be lost. He knew that the same thing that had saved him had also accomplished this beaching of the *Hattie.*

If she had been a deep-draft keel boat she would not have reached the beach but would have been stopped some distance from the shore, the wind would have laid her over on her side, and she would have filled with water. She would have taken such a battering from the brutal winds and surf that her crew would have had no choice but to swim for it, and their chances would have been very slim. In a short time she would have broken up and her cargo would have been scattered, coming ashore as flotsam and jetsam, the property of anyone who found it.

But both boats had centerboards that had moved upward when they encountered the bottom and this had put the *Hattie* on the beach and got the *Albatross* across the bar. But John Talbott knew there had been something else, even more important, that had contributed to his safe passage of the point. He had been saved by Toby's desperate change of course to keep the mainsail filled. The sudden change had carried him out to the end of the bar and he had scraped across, leaving a few coats of copper paint in a furrow in the sand, but nothing more. He doubted if he had been in less than four and a half feet of water, but with her board partially down, and heavily loaded, the *Albatross* had needed a foot or two more to clear completely. But he had made it; the *Albatross* was still seaworthy, still plunging along in the gale. With Toby on deck he had a chance now to get under the shelter of the Cliffs of Calvert and enter the river.

He stooped to the deck and picked up the wet, snow-covered cigar that had been knocked from his mouth as he fell against the wheel. It was still almost its original length and he knew it had been long extinguished, but he had held it clenched tightly in his teeth for a long, long time. He knocked the snow off it against a spoke of the wheel and shoved it back into his mouth. As he did he detected a dark shadow on the foredeck, framed against the whiteness of the snow. And the shadow was moving. At the same time he saw a head beginning to emerge from the aft cabin. He realized that his crew was reviving. The effect of the Dover's Powder and, more than that, he was sure, the sound of the centerboard's scraping on the bottom had restored them to a somewhat shaky state of usefulness.

The wind was now northwest for certain and they would have to jibe now or run away from their destination. It was so close, and the choice was now his to make, whereas only minutes before there had been no choice at all. The odds might have shifted in his favor. Perhaps with Toby's strength to offset the weakness of the others, they could manage. "Stand by to jibe," he shouted, and the men moved off sluggishly to execute the order.

Once safely around, the main boom now on the port side, the jib set and trimmed, he headed for the lee of the cliffs, where he knew he could count on relatively smooth water the rest of the way. Gradually the wind seemed to ease and the water became smoother. Without really thinking about what he was doing, without having the idea firmly fixed in his mind, he eased her up toward the wind, calling for the men to trim her close-hauled.

"Get the lead line, Toby! Go forward and heave it! Give me soundings every minute!"

"What are you going to do, skipper?"

"I'm going back to Cove Point! Tom Webster might need our help!"

Toby got the lead line and went forward. He stood near the bow on the starboard side and heaved the lead far out in front of the boat. "Deep four and soft!" he shouted.

"Stand by to go about!" he heard the skipper shout.

"Half three and soft!"

97

"Stand by!"

"Quarter less twain and hard!"

"Hard-alee! Smartly now!" The skipper threw the helm down and the *Albatross* came up into the wind, her sails flapping, the water splashing confusedly around her. She fell off on the other tack and gathered way through the waves.

"Mark twain!" Toby shouted. . . .

"Half twain and soft!" he called. *What are we going to do when we get there?* he thought. *It'll be tough trying to get ashore. We'll have to launch the yawl boat and she's covered and the cover is frozen. The tackle's probably frozen too. But we've got to help if we can.*

He threw the lead again, far out in front of the boat, taking in the line as the boat moved forward until the line was straight up and down, checking the marker on the rope in the glow from the starboard running light, lifting the weight at the end of the rope and dropping it again, feeling it suck loose from the mud on the bottom. "Half twain and soft!"

On a night like this, Toby thought, *there's bound to be somebody awake in there, but you can't be sure they would even know what happened with all this wind blowing and the snow. Maybe nobody was looking and nobody heard those masts go.*

"Mark twain and hard, Skipper!"

There was a flash of light ahead just off the port bow. Then there was another one. He could hear the surf pounding on the far side of the point up ahead. Now he could see the heart of the light, which never went completely dark between the flashes. The *Albatross* continued on her course.

"Quarter less twain!"

Ten and a half feet, Toby thought. *He can't go much closer. He's got to heave to right now.* And then he saw the lights. They were moving and they were down on the point beyond the lighthouse. He quickly counted five of them. He checked the lead again. "Ten feet! Ten feet!" He tried to control the alarm he knew was in his voice. The centerboard was down all the way now and this was getting pretty close.

"Hard-alee!"

She came up into the wind and the skipper turned the wheel over to Ed Shorter. He told him to hold her into the wind and ran forward to the starboard railing alongside Toby. "Ahoy!" he shouted. "Ahoy there!"

He saw the lights stop moving. He could not see anyone, but he sensed they had stopped what they were doing and were looking in his direction. He estimated they were less than fifty yards away. He heard the sound of shouting.

"John! Is that you, John?" The voice was clear coming down the wind and he recognized it as Tom Webster's.

"Yes! Yes!" he shouted. "He made it! Oh, thank God, he made it!"

"We are all right! Cargo is safe! Go to Solomons! Don't try to land! Tell Bob Cook to come for cargo tomorrow! Do you hear?"

"I hear you!" He turned to Toby. "Nothing we can do here," he said. "Let's back the jib and get out of here."

The *Albatross* dropped off away from the point. Soon they were under the lee of the cliffs again, in calmer water, making good speed toward Drum Point. But there was a feeling of profound anguish when Talbott considered Captain Webster's loss. It meant that there would be one less sailboat on the Bay. The death of a sailboat of eighty-five feet was a tragic loss, not only for the money she represented to her owner, the means of livelihood to her crew, but more than that, because she was irreplaceable. With steam carrying a larger share of the available cargo every year, no one would finance the construction of a sailboat anymore, except a yacht or an oyster boat.

There were tears in his eyes as he watched Drum

Point Light appear out of the snow and then change from red to white just off his starboard bow, telling him it was safe to turn into the mouth of the river.

The *Albatross* lay alongside the oyster house and sank lower and lower into the water as the oysters were shoveled down into her hold. The wind was stiff out of the northwest; the ground was a brilliant white with its new blanket of snow on top of the older, gray snow, and there was not a cloud in the sky. The sun had melted the snow and ice from the decks and rigging of the *Albatross,* and for still another reason Toby was glad the sun was shining. The temperature was now eighteen. If the sun had not been shining so brilliantly the *Albatross* would have remained shrouded in snow and ice, but more than that it was downright comfortable, actually warm, in the sunshine as he huddled down behind the aft cabin trunk with the skipper and watched the workmen loading the oysters into her hold. It was the first time he had been able to relax since he had rushed on deck at almost six in the morning.

The day had been filled with furious activity and the men had worked themselves into a gradually improving state of well-being, sweating the poison out of their rugged systems as they worked in spite of the cold.

First they had unloaded the coal, doing most of the work themselves before the arrival of a group of dockhands to take over. Toby and the skipper had worked right along with Ed and Harry, doing most of the heavy work at the beginning, but as the morning wore on and the men worked up a good sweat they gradually improved.

Then, after the boat was unloaded and the last of the coal dust was swept up and thrown overboard and the holds were made suitable for the oysters, they towed the big schooner across the mouth of the harbor—about a hundred yards—to the oyster house, where they lay alongside to pick up their return cargo. Shortly after they left the steamer wharf they saw Robert Cook and a crew of eighteen men leave for the mouth of the river in the Cook pungey, bound for Cove Point with three stout skiffs in tow to pick up the cargo of the *Hattie*.

And now, as the *Albatross* reached nearly her full load, they watched the sails of the pungey come from behind the point of land, saw her sail behind the spindly legs of the screw-pile lighthouse at Drum Point, tack across to the far shore, and come about to make for the harbor's entrance. She was coming very fast, close-hauled, heeling prettily as she came in under the lee of the land. She rounded up, dropped her sails and, with just a handkerchief of cloth on her, ran downwind to the Cook wharf.

After several minutes a skiff put out and moved across the harbor toward the *Albatross*. Toby could make out the big shape of Captain Webster sitting on the stern seat and recognized several other members of the *Hattie*'s crew. He and the skipper walked around to the starboard railing, and Toby caught the painter of the skiff as it was thrown up. Tom Webster looked up and smiled. "Hello, John. Wonder if you could give us passage back to Baltimore?"

He was rising as he said it, assuming the answer that he knew would come. He stepped on the middle seat, grasped the rail, stepped on the rubbing strake, and heaved himself up and over the railing.

"How are you, Cap'n Tom?" Toby said.

"Oh, I'm pretty good, I guess. As good as you can expect for an old man who spent the night with his rear end in the water. God, what a night!" He looked around at the men loading the oysters into the hold. "I'm glad you didn't have any trouble, Toby."

There was silence from the group of men from both crews who had clustered around. And then Toby started to laugh. "No trouble! No trouble? Wait'll you hear what happened to us."

He started the story and was interrupted by each

member of the crew of the *Albatross* at least four or five times. Expressions of growing admiration spread across the faces of the *Hattie*'s crew. When the story was finished the men all stood quietly for a moment. Tom Webster turned away and stood at the rail looking out over the harbor, quietly shaking his head. John Talbott walked over and put his hand on the old captain's shoulder. "What about your cargo, Tom? Anything we can do to give you a hand?"

Tom Webster shook his head. "That's mighty nice of you, truly it is, John, but it ain't necessary. Bob Cook got up there pretty quick and they loaded right much on the pungey. There's still more, but he bought the whole thing right where it lay, and he gave me a damn good price for it too. Better'n I'd have asked."

"What about the *Hattie*?"

"Oh, she's a wreck. Total loss. Nothing worth repairing or salvaging. You'll see her when we go by. I got her clock and compass and a few other things, but that was all there was. But her old hull held together long enough to keep the cargo from going adrift. God bless her for that."

The sun was low in the sky when the *Albatross* came out from under the headland and met the force

105

of the breeze as it jumped off the shore and moved across the half mile of open water. She was close-hauled, driving, and carrying a bone in her teeth as the white water curled away from her bow. She was bound for home. As she swept regally past Cove Point the men stood silently at the port rail and regarded the wreck of the *Hattie,* which lay in the shallow water just north of the point, close by the lighthouse. Spray broke over the wreck as the waves pounded at it. Several of the men had tears in their eyes and made no attempt to hide them; others sighed deeply, looked searchingly at each other and shook their heads.

Both crews had vivid memories of the night before, but the crew of the *Hattie* remembered most clearly the way Captain Webster was hauled out of the swirling, frigid water by the hair of his great white beard, muttered his thanks, then climbed right back up on the wreck and stayed there soaking wet the rest of the night in order to protect his salvage rights. In the morning they had watched him work along with the rest of them and with Cook's men to transfer the cargo into the pungey's boats.

The time was 4:55, and as Seaman John Davis walked out of the radio shack he turned to watch the

Albatross go by. He also looked for a long time at the wreckage strewn along the beach. At this time of the day he would normally have been fast asleep, but he had been too excited by the events of the early-morning hours to even think of going to sleep. He was still elated over his first experience involving a rescue. He remembered it all clearly from the very first moment.

At 5:52 that morning Seaman Davis had been shaking down the clinkers in the potbellied stove in the radio shack. He had just come in out of the snow with a full scuttle of coal and set it on the floor beside the stove. When he finished, and the ashes and clinkers had settled to the bottom of the stove, he opened the draft to give the fire a chance to catch up, and then slowly stood, lifting the coal scuttle with one hand and opening the front door of the stove with the other.

The mere physical act of standing brought him face-to-face with the northeast window of the radio shack and face-to-face with what he knew was the starboard running light of something where nothing had any right to be. He stood transfixed and stared in disbelief for a split second, unable to move, unable to believe what he was seeing, and then the light vanished. Then came the muffled, splintering

107

crash. The coal scuttle hit the floor. He reached for the pull cord on the alarm bell, jerked it as hard as he could a half dozen times, then opened the door and dashed out into the night.

He was proud that he had been the one to sound the alarm, and only he and Tom Webster would ever know how close the captain had come to drowning. Davis had grabbed him by the hair of his beard and pulled him out of the way of a large piece of the main boom that was being hurled directly at his head by the roaring surf. It had been very close.

And he had thrilled at the courage of that redoubtable old man who climbed back up on the wreck to hold his salvage rights. This was the kind of thrilling thing he had only read about in books, and here it was happening before his very eyes.

No wonder he couldn't sleep. And then the pungey had come to take away the cargo, and he had watched as the men fought the skiffs through the breakers and moved the barrels of coal oil. It had been a thrilling day, but the thing that had impressed him the most had been looking up in the midst of all the turmoil and seeing the running lights of another boat in close to shore. The fact that someone would dare to maneuver such a large boat that close inshore in such weather was an act of courage and skill he would never forget.

He watched the *Albatross* sail by the point, thinking how beautiful she was, knowing that the two boats had come down the Bay together the night before, and wondering how one had wrecked and the other had sailed safely by. Two words ran through his mind, a lesson learned from a text and dramatically brought home before his very eyes. Two words that, in his young opinion, made the difference between the wreckage strewn on the beach and the schooner passing the point. He had read them many times, in fact he had read them again only the night before: *Eternal Vigilance.*

The two captains stood at the rail near the stern, apart from the rest of the men. They had not spoken since they sighted the wreckage. There was nothing to say. The look on Tom Webster's face was one of utter desolation.

Suddenly he sighed deeply and said, "Well, she was insured, thank God, but no amount of money in this world will ever replace her."

"Well, that's something to be thankful for, God knows. But it isn't much compared to the luck I had." The word seemed to slip out before he knew it, but there seemed to be no other explanation for his survival.

Webster shook his head. "I don't know, John. I just don't know. I reckon there's no such thing as luck when you get right down to it. It doesn't really exist, except maybe ashore in a poker game or a dice game. All my life I've believed in it, even counted on it to some extent, but I'll never thank it or curse it again. The day before we left Baltimore I signed on for that captain's berth on that new steamer Weems is building at Sparrows Point. They want me to take her long enough to whip a crew into shape, which is just about long enough for me; but I had to take one more shot at this Bay in a sailboat, figuring my luck would see me through somehow in a situation I knew damn well was risky. On the spur of the moment I decided to go along, counting on my luck. You decided to go after figuring out all of the angles. I know you think you were lucky, but I'll just be damned if I'll say that luck had anything to do with the best job of single-handed sailing I've ever seen or heard about."

John Talbott shook his head. "It wasn't very well planned and that's for certain."

"You've been planning it all your life, John. You know that in the back of your mind you have considered this thing happening and what you'd do. All of us have. No, I just figured I was too lucky to ever have anything like this happen to me."

They fell silent. Since the wreck Talbott had been a sober, chastened man, a man struggling deep within himself to determine what had happened to his entire outlook. He was stronger and more secure than ever as to his ability, and perhaps it really hadn't been luck; nevertheless, for the first time in his life he was acutely aware that there were some things over which a man has absolutely no control, no matter how carefully he plans.

Having a sick crew, being left alone on the deck to fight singlehanded for stark survival, experiencing a shift of wind that had threatened to carry him away from the light that had shepherded him through the horrible night—what cruel circumstances they had seemed at the time! But these things, and the arrival of Toby on deck at just the right minute, were the things that had saved him. He remembered cursing Tom Webster and his luck. Had Talbott's crew been on deck to handle the sails, the *Albatross* would have been wreckage on the beach only a few yards from the *Hattie,* her cargo perhaps lost beyond recovery.

This had not been the first time he had been

forced to face disaster, but it was the first time he had ever faced it so completely alone. And he *had* faced it, fought it, and won. The knowledge of this gave him great strength, but he knew that he would never again scoff at men who smoked their pipes, drank their hot buttered rum, and praised or cursed their luck. There was a lesson to be learned here, and somehow he must see that Toby had learned it.

Chapter Eight

THE FOLLOWING EVENING, in the warmth of his own dining room, with a good dinner of fried oysters under his belt and a cup of coffee before him, he leaned back in his chair and grinned at Toby. The children were playing in the living room and Laura was quietly enjoying the presence of her husband.

"You know, son, it seems to me that a man only gets a certain amount of luck during his life on this earth. And it seems like you don't always get what seems to be your fair share every time. Sometimes you get a little, sometimes you get a lot. And sometimes, when you really need it, you don't get any at all. But everybody needs a little luck now and then, and maybe the Good Lord knows this and sees to it that we get some. But you never know when it's coming, so you can't count on it coming when you need it.

"Now you take Tom Webster. He believes in luck as much as any man I ever knew. Says he's changed, but I don't believe that. To a certain extent he counts on it—but only to a certain extent, no matter what he might say. And he's never been a man who stood around waiting for it, and when it doesn't come he isn't one to curse his luck and stand around helpless. He's smart enough and brave enough, and has enough experience so he just keeps right on going in spite of everything, knowing his luck will catch up with him eventually and he can take care of himself until it does.

"But the person who stands around all day long doing nothing because he thinks he's going to get a lucky break tomorrow, well, he's in for a bad time. Usually he's still standing around tomorrow. And the next day as well. He's counting on something that may never happen. And the longer he stands around the less chance he's got of ever seeing anything at all in the way of luck. The person who waltzes through life counting on luck never really has enough luck to amount to anything. And when he does get a little he's usually in no position to take advantage of it. He's just fooling himself.

"It seems to me that a man who really can take advantage of the normal amount of luck a man gets in the normal course of events is a man who works hard, plans carefully, and doesn't keep waiting for a lucky break. But when he gets one he can usually turn it into a big break because he's in a position to really take advantage of it.

"What I'm really trying to say, son, is that it seems to me that you make your own luck lots of times, and even if you don't, being ready for it can make a lot of difference in how much luck you seem to get."

About the Author

KENNETH F. BROOKS, JR., was born in Washington, D. C., on July 12, 1921, and has lived in the metropolitan area of Washington all of his life. He attended local elementary and junior high schools and Virginia Episcopal School, a boys' prep school in Lynchburg, Virginia. Between the time he finished school and the beginning of World War II he worked as a copy boy on the *Washington Evening Star.*

Mr. Brooks entered the service as an Aviation Cadet, studied Aerial Navigation and, upon completion of the course, was commissioned a second lieutenant with the rating of navigator. As such he flew twenty-nine combat missions over Europe in Martin B26 planes. He was wounded on the twenty-ninth mission and returned to the United States for treatment. His decorations included the Silver Star, Air Medal with four clusters, and the Purple Heart. Following hospitalization he served in the Air Transport Command, ferrying aircraft to India and the South Pacific. At the end of the war he was based in Miami, flying on a regularly scheduled military transport run between Miami and Casablanca.

Mr. Brooks has deep family roots in the Chesapeake Bay area, his ancestors being among its first settlers. On his mother's side of the family, his ancestors were steamboat people. His great-uncle, James Russell Gourley, was a steamboat captain who served fifty-one years with the Weems Line and was Commodore of the Weems Fleet at the time the line was sold. His grandfather was a purser on many Chesapeake Bay steamers.

Much of Mr. Brooks' childhood was spent on the water. His uncle had a sailboat, then a cabin cruiser, and Mr. Brooks spent his summers on board. He also visited his grandmother's farm on the Patuxent River. As a boy he learned to sail, row, oyster, fish and generally feel at home on the water.

Between 1964 and 1967 Mr. Brooks was manager of press and publicity for the Washington Convention and Visitors Bureau, writing much of the promotion material for the National Cherry Blossom Festival, the Pageant of Peace, and other tourist promotion activities of the Bureau. He is now writing full-time and attending classes at the Northern Virginia Center for Continuing Education of the University of Virginia.

Kenneth Brooks is married to the former Amy Wilson of Milwaukee, and is the father of four children, two boys and two girls. He has been active in Boy Scouts, and was the first president of the Yorktown High School Boosters Club, an organization formed to start a schoolboy crew at Yorktown High School in Arlington. He is also a member of the Chesapeake Bay Maritime Museum at St. Michaels, Maryland.

His favorite hobbies are camping and sailing. His sailboat, an eleven foot Sea Snark, was given to him on his forty-eighth birthday by his eldest daughter.

About the Illustrator

JOSHUA TOLFORD has a background of fine and technical art. As a painter, he came to Rockport, Massachusetts, studied with Anthony Thieme, then, with his artist wife, established and maintained the Tolford Gallery, before moving to Boston, then to Carlisle, Massachusetts, and more recently to Acton in that state.

His technical training was acquired on various jobs—as a patent draftsman and as technical illustrator for such firms as American Optical Company, Allied Research, and General Electric. For the last ten years he has been a technical artist with Arthur D. Little, Inc., a research firm in Cambridge, Massachusetts, where he is called on to do conceptual drawings of anything from a moon suit to a gear drive for a crystal-growing furnace.

As an illustrator of children's books, he has a list of twenty-five titles, on all subjects. He illustrated and designed *Pioneer Iron Works*, which was written by Mary Stetson Clarke, and published by Chilton in 1968. It won first place as the best illustrated and designed juvenile in The Philadelphia Book Show in 1969.

106		

106 Michael		APR 1 1976